CLOCKTOWER BOOKS

Terror in My Arms

A Dark San Diego Crime Thriller

By

John T. Cullen

Clocktower Books, San Diego

www.clocktowerbooks.com

The night the ordeal was all finally over—as the SDPD patrol car speeded to the hospital with flashing lights through a splattering rain—Sylvie Bancroft sat in the back seat, still in shock, and recalled the exact moment when Rob Turlock had come into her life.

It was silent in the police cruiser. *Blessed silence. Peace.* What she most needed now.

She was done crying. Everything now was happening in a dream, as she sat with both bandaged hands in her lap.

She'd come back from the brink of death.

Was it really over now, finally?

The San Diego police car smelled stale inside, like a thousand nights, like old cigarettes and stale coffee, old ashes and old traumas. She pulled the blanket tight around her shoulders, over her soaked clothing, and shivered. Passing street lights streaked bars of light and dark through her eyes, over her lap, over her clasped and trembling hands.

She remembered how bright and warm the sunshine had been that day so recently!

She'd been a software engineer for ten years, and the past four of those years as an outside consultant had been the best of her life. She was a woman on the go, worked hard, delivered on schedule, got paid well, and treasured both her independence and her good reputation. At three in afternoon, a Wednesday, she walked into her client's door carrying the CD-ROM with 10,000 lines of QA-ready code and a 150-page user manual that she'd subcontracted to a good friend.

A man said to her: "You have such a glow on your face!" and she ignored him as she swept through the lobby with both arms full.

She ignored him, and did not think about him again until she was on her way out. Men came on to women, and that was how it worked, except for the maneuvering women did to be in the way when they wanted to be. It was nice sometimes to be admired, but often it wasn't. Right now, with the red-haired man in the lobby, who did have an exceptionally big smile and coolly controlled, sincere yet winking eyes, she did not have time to make a judgment. She clearly had not maneuvered into his way; rather she almost ran him over on her way to the elevator. She was interested only in working 14 hours a day for four months deliver on schedule. She had her own annoyance rate with wolf-whistlers and awkward guys to deal with, as did every woman, and Sylvie knew her strengths and weaknesses all too intensely, as did most women. Her rate of being propositioned was about average; maybe if she flattered herself, a little above. She was slender, with a fresh face and long black hair. When she dressed up for a dinner or a dance—with contact lenses instead of the heavy horn eyeglasses, with the right makeup and a gown and high heels—she'd been called really pretty. Once or twice maybe beautiful. In her free time, she jogged and surfed and bicycled, which kept her complexion ruddy and glowing. Actually, despite the French surname, she also had some extremely recessive alleles for dark skin by way of Cuba and perhaps Africa, but her hair was straight and her eyes were gray-blue; anyway, that helped her look tanned without the U.V. risk from the sun. She was a vegetarian, with a weakness for chocolate.

As she stepped off the elevator, $15,000 check firmly in her purse, she nearly ran into a wall of flowers. Actually, it was a large bouquet, and she stopped in her tracks. Red roses. They lowered, revealing the face of the man with the seductive eyes. "Hi!" His teeth were clean and big. "You have such a glow." He shook the flowers. "I took the liberty of buying these so I could learn why you look so utterly radiant."

She felt the still-wet, paper-wrapped roses against her arm, the flowers damp against her exposed skin in the v of her blouse. She wore, that day, her corporate garb: dark jacket and skirt, white silk blouse, tiny gold necklace; black pumps, conservative nylons, light make-up. "No way," she said, pushing the flowers back.

"I won't take no for an answer." He stood aside holding the roses, and she saw in his eyes that he would run after her.

She stopped in amazement, stamped one foot lightly, and stared at him. His gaze was somehow a little hooded, but so confident, so crisp and direct, so guileless, that instead of telling him off, she started to laugh.

"I wanted to let you tell me. I'm a good listener." He held the roses out to her. "I want to learn what it is that makes you glow like that. I'm in sales, you know. Maybe I can bottle it, patent it, make the world a shiny and wonderful place."

"You are really too much. Not a chance." She felt herself weakening. If anything was radiant it was the check in her purse.

He saw her weakening. How did this type of man do that? Was he naturally endowed with an ability to decipher body language, to read minds, to read the widening and narrowing of a woman's irises as she wavered in indecision, between desire and negation?

"What do you want?"

"Your phone number. Lunch. Take the flowers."

She shook her head. They were exquisitely fragrant, so deeply rouge that the shadows in their folds made them look as if they were edged with black velvet.

He extended his arms from his sides, roses waving in the air. He was as tall as she, athletically slender like she, wearing a long-sleeved white shirt and conservative business suit. His expensive shoes were mahogany loafers whose tassels somehow told her he really was in sales. "If you won't take them, what am I going to do with a dozen red roses?"

"Give them to your girlfriend." She tittered. "To your wife."

"I'm between girlfriends, and my ex is just a friend."

Sylvie nodded. "Where do you work?" Oh God, she was letting him talk her into something. There was something about him she wasn't sure of, but he was really quite attractive, an assertive red-head. She judged him to be about her age—thirty—and there were some hints of life's stress hardened what must long have been a baby face.

"I'm in sales. Guthrie Turlock Donaldson." Like a magician, he flicked the index and middle fingers of his free hand, and a business card appeared between the fingers. He seemed to do things with snap. She held the card in both hands and read it, her contacts floating loosely on her eyeballs and making her vision blur a little. The card had names and phone numbers and e-mail addresses and web information. The trade name GTD was embossed in the middle. Under that it said Rob Turlock, Director of Sales.

She put the card in her purse. "I'll think about it."

"Can I think about it too?"

She turned to leave, and he followed. "I'll need your number though, to successfully think about it."

She stopped, laughed, and gave him a card. Wow. This guy was a good act. She wasn't sure if she found herself attracted to him, but he seemed interesting.

That was it, she told herself on the way through the parking garage under the building, he seemed interesting. Maybe he could be fun. Maybe lunch. A movie. She had two weeks before her next gig started, and maybe he liked surfing.

She actually forgot him as she started her little red Mercedes convertible and thought about surfing. She suddenly got the idea to drive up to Solana Beach tomorrow with her surfboard and wetsuit. No, maybe down to Coronado, within sight of Mexico, where a mile of Pacific breakers boomed onto sand that glittered gold with silica.

She presented her validated parking ticket to the booth attendant. He nodded and she put on her sunglasses and pulled into the April sunshine on Washington Street. Just then, Rob Turlock drove slowly by in a beautiful, glossy moss-green Porsche. A white-shirted arm waved. His teeth flashed a smile. She gave a little wave, just wriggly fingers, and nodded as he drove off.

Reality, however, presented itself in the form of her condo, which had not had a proper cleaning in six weeks. When she was busy like she'd been, Sylvie called a service to come in and clean once a week. This time around, she hadn't even had time to do that much. Before she could relax at all, Sylvie must clean the entire place—three bedrooms, a bath, kitchen, and living room. Her single-car garage below was always clean except for the junk wall. That was where she stored "stuff."

In the middle of all this, as she wore the traditional and probably legally mandated yellow gloves, the phone rang. She put down the mop and the bucket with which she was headed to the bathroom. Running one bare forearm over her forehead, she picked up the portable phone in the kitchen with the other.

"Hello, Sylvie, this is Rob Turlock."

"Oh yes," she said noncommittally. Her heart beat a little faster, and she stepped onto the little patio. Good that he couldn't see her now, wearing her old Bermuda shorts and a faded Good Times in Ensenada t-shirt. She wasn't wearing a bra, but her breasts were small and firm, and never in the way. She actually owned a few very frou-frou white cotton bras with silk ruffles, but mostly she wore athletic bras. She sprawled on one of her white plastic chairs and put her legs on the other, expecting a seductive conversation. She was ready to parry, to hold her own, to dictate terms.

"So," Rob said, "I've been thinking about it, as I'm sure you have, and I've successfully concluded that I really ought to ask you to come surfing with me tomorrow."

"What!" she squealed. "This is too much. You must read minds. I can't believe it." Suddenly, her two week time off was starting to fill in with interesting activities. She went back into the house and began to feel a warm glow inside as she dusted around the vase that held her dozen roses.

The next day, Rob Turlock swept by in his green Porsche and picked her up. "I had a little trouble finding your place," he said as she climbed in. He clicked his white teeth on the ear stems of his horn-rimmed sunglasses. "But I was determined to find you."

"Shall I bring my board?"
"I don't have my rack up. Let's rent."
"Okay!"
She climbed in, giving him a sidelong examination. He put his sunglasses on, shifted gears with a tolerant, practiced look, and slid into traffic. He had small hands, she saw, pale and freckled, and a big head. Not a big head, a biggish head, she amended. He was downright handsome, in his tight jeans, deck shoes, and white denim shirt. There was

something calculating about him, but that must be the salesman in him. Size people up. Schmooze. Close the deal. That was how he got to drive this expensive car.

"I thought we'd go to San Clemente."

"I thought we were going to Solana Beach."

"Oh, the surfing's better up the coast this time of year. It's not actually up the coast but west, further out in the ocean. Catch more waves out there."

"Okay." She put her sunglasses on and relaxed, letting the fresh air and sunshine flow around her along with really clear wrap-around music from an incredibly good stereo system. By coincidence, her favorite radio station was on, playing a mix of contemporary jazz and classic rock. "Each of these songs is so great! I love them all, and I've never heard them this clear."

"European engineering." He glanced at her sideways, not smiling, as if not sure she understood.

"So are you an engineer?"

"No, I told you, sales."

"And what do you sell?"

"Big machinery. Farm equipment, the generators that power up an airliner, that kind of stuff."

She remembered the card. "Who are Guthrie and Donaldson?"

"Partners." He looked tanned and suddenly businesslike, as if running the complexities of his business through his mind while dressed to play on the beach. "Guthrie is old—50—and he inherited from his father. Donaldson is my age. Guthrie's the engineer, but he's fat and gross and can't sell. Donaldson runs the business. He's a little wind-up twit. Dots his i's and crosses his t's."

"Sounds like you guys don't like each other."

"I can't say we're crazy about each other. But we're a team that works. Two hundred million in gross revenues last year, huh?"

"Hmmm." She noticed a copy of TheWall Street Journal on the floor. She unfolded it—it was a week old—and smoothed out the financial section. She scanned down the New York Stock Exchange listings, column by column, to where GTD should be. It wasn't. "You guys aren't listed."

"We don't trade publicly. We obtain our funding from private investors, Sylvie. Do you know much about finance?"

"Some. My minor was accounting, but I'm afraid I'm just your basic software engineer."

"And a beautiful one at that."

"Oh come now."

"We have very large institutional investors, like insurance companies, and some private investors." He named several big names that she associated with fabulous fortunes. "All those people," he said, "are not going to gamble in the sort of bull pit, if you will, that the hoi polloi throw their money. These are old fortunes, and we're rock solid."

On the beach near San Clemente, they ran down hand in hand to the water. There she pulled her hand away, and he seemed respectful of her distance. He was like that all day. They swam, surfed, swam again, ran in the sand, collapsed tiredly, napped in the sun, then went for lunch in a fine little restaurant near the beach. They drank margaritas and ate from a salad bar that included chopped fresh-roasted chicken breast and a whole variety of good things. He paid by credit card and then they strolled arm in arm on the beach. Never once did his hands roam where they shouldn't, not even a fingertip.

At dusk, he kissed her lightly on the mouth as the sun set in a fiery ball over the Pacific Ocean. She kept a fairly neutral position, with her hands against his arms and her face upraised, but her eyes open. He laughed almost imperceptibly, inwardly, and shook her very gently as if to loosen her up. His inward laugh infected her and she laughed too, closing her eyes as his lips touched hers. She sensed the strength in him, and the holding back. She felt the cords in his arms and imagined he could be very passionate. For the first time, that thought nibbled interestedly at the wall of her resistance. Not resistance, she decided, but indifference borne of hard work and long hours. Too much. Too much. Gotta loosen up, she thought, I'll only live once.

In the car on the way home, she said: "Thanks for a wonderful day."

"I really enjoyed it too."

She stared out at the passing lights on Interstate 5 headed south into San Diego and thought out loud. "I have two weeks before I start a really big project, and you won't see me for a few months."

"Oh?"

"Yes. I'm going to burn the candle at both ends and then take the rest of the year off." The thought filled her with delight and she burst forth: "If you're around, maybe we can take a trip. Cabo San Lucas—." She caught herself and wanted to bite her tongue, realizing she'd let down her guard.

"I own a home here, Sylvie. I'll be around." He smiled slightly, and there was nothing lecherous in it. "What if we were just to run away together now? Tonight?"

She laughed. What a funny thing to say. She glanced over and he was laughing too. "Show me your house. I want to see your house." She slapped her hand on her seat between her knees for emphasis. "I'm curious."

He looked at his watch.

Her heart sank. "Oh no, not if you have to go somewhere."

"I'm sorry, that was rude. It's just—I have to fly out in the morning to Chicago. Please forgive me."

"It's okay."

"No really, I didn't mean to be rude. I'll give you a quick tour and then take you home."

"No," she said, but she was curious. Partly, she wanted to see if there was any evidence he was married and maybe just playing around. Girlfriend—that wouldn't bother her. Wife—that she wouldn't tolerate. Partly, too, she wanted to test him a little more before she could trust him.

The house was wonderful. Nestled in a dead-end street high in the hills of La Jolla, the house had a panoramic view of the Pacific Ocean. As she and Rob drove up, the house seemed perched just under the sky. If they climbed any higher, they'd be flying. A full moon cast its cool light over clean concrete walks and driveways. Lush vegetation choking the house looked black. Thick walls and hedges on either side shut out nosy neighbors, if there were any. The black wrought-iron gates were open, and in each was welded a large T. The garage door slid open as they approached, and Rob drove right into the garage. "What a beautiful home," she said sincerely.

"I take good care of it," Rob said getting out with a jingle of keys. "It represents everything I've worked for in my life, and I'm quite proud of it."

The garage had room for four cars, but only two spaces were actually in use. She pointed to a light blue Italian sports car. Instinctively she felt it must have a feminine owner. "Whose is that?"

"That was my ex-wife's," he said. "I'm afraid we had a somewhat bitter divorce, and I got to keep her car." Before Sylvie could reply, he seemed to anger slightly. He rose up on the balls of his feet and counted on his fingers. "Don't worry, she got the silverware, the good china, her jewelry, some of the furniture, everything but my gold fillings."

"I'm sorry." She felt taken aback.

"No, I'm sorry. That was rude again. No need for you to worry about my old private stuff."

"Okay. Well anyway, it's a nice house." She noted the dark recesses of the garage. Where the other cars would be, there were ceiling-high wooden racks.

Some contained stored clothing carriers on hangers, others books, others yet boxes that looked as if they might be full of letters and papers. Along the far wall was a huge collection of wine bottles that pointed outward from wooden slats.

Rob led the way, showing her some of the house's twelve rooms, two full baths, and two half baths. They didn't go upstairs, where he said were five bedrooms and a library. The tidy white kitchen gleamed with soft fluorescent lighting partially covered by stained-glass designs. The enormous living room, which was deeply carpeted with heavy couches and chairs done in a thick wheat design offset by brass handles, had several picture windows overlooking the ocean. "Glass of wine?" Rob asked.

"Thanks, just a small one."

He poured them each half-glasses. "Got to drive yet," he explained.

She pointed to the many pictures all around. "Who are these people?"

"Family. I don't have any children, and my ex is out of the picture. I have several brothers and sisters, and they have children. I won't bother naming them all right now, but I promise you, if you stick around, I'll eventually make you memorize all their names."

They walked through the living room, up some steps, and out onto the back lawn. "Oh Rob, this is so beautiful." The house lights were dim, and the full moon rode high, casting chairs and a diving board and a golf cart and a parked sailboat into shadowless relief. The lawn curved away, as if its curvature were that of the world. From this house she felt a power emanate; she could almost reach her arms out and move the ships around that lay full of lights on the ocean. Or reach up and turn around a large prop plane that droned overhead with winking signals, as if it were a child's toy.

"Watch your step!" Rob said suddenly.

She nearly fell into a hole in the lawn, and Rob caught her around the waist. As she recovered, he released his grip on her, and she felt embarrassed. "I was so taken with your view that I fell over my own two feet. What is this hole for?" The hole was Robed with slender wooden poles joined fence-like with white twine about two feet off the ground, and someone had hung little warning rags all around. The hole was about ten feet long and two feet wide.

"I'm putting in new sprinklers. The old ones no longer work."

They stood at the rim of the hill, where the lights of other houses peeked mysteriously from among huge trees below. They watched the ocean a while longer, big thing like an animal with its belly pregnant with mysteries.

Rob drove her home. As she got out, he leaned close, and she planted a brief kiss on his lips and touched his nose.

Next morning she finally got to the bank with her check. Then she went to visit Claire Morelos, her personnel rep at Moorage Technical Temps. Claire was a large, pleasant woman with thick, glossy black hair. "Hi, Sylvie. I hear you did a wonderful job for our client."

"Thanks. I felt pretty good about it. I also felt good taking the check to the bank." Claire had left Sylvie's check with the client to save Sylvie a trip to MTT's offices.

"We felt good cutting it for you. So are you almost ready to go back to work?"

"Oh please, I need a week or two to sleep."

"Those 14 hour days get to you, eh?" Claire checked her schedule. "Yes, looks like you can pick up a three to six month assignment starting about two weeks from now. Or would you rather rest a little and see what we get in the door a little later?"

Sylvie briefly thought it over. "No, I want one more good juicy job this year. I want to take November and December off and visit my folks back East. I also might take a trip to Cabo then. I'd rather take the job."

"Good. I'll put you down," Claire said with a flourish of her fountain pen. "You have two weeks to rest up and enjoy yourself before we throw you back into the cauldron. What are you going to do with your time." She leaned close and whispered: "Anybody special in your life?"

Sylvie grinned weakly. She knew she had a reputation as a workaholic, which was unfounded, because she did like her free time a lot. It was true that she had trouble meeting or keeping boyfriends because of her lifestyle. Her goal was to finish paying off the condo before taking a regular position and possibly looking around at the eligible men. She was attractive and had no worries about not finding someone.

"You do!" Claire said. "I can see the light in your eyes."

"Just a flirtation." Sylvie rose quickly, to head off Claire's imaginative mind. "Just right for a week or two, and then it's back to business as usual."

"Make the best of it!" Claire chimed as Sylvie left.

In the morning, Sylvie did a little more testing. She called the number on the card. "Guthrie Turlock Donaldson," said a crisp, business-like middle-aged woman.

"Hi, is Mr. Turlock in?"

"I'll check. Hold please." After a moment: "I'm sorry, he's not in the office at the moment. Would you like to leave a message on his voice mail?"

"Er—no thanks."

She hung up, feeling relieved. She drove the ten minutes to La Jolla and drove past the address on the card. Sure enough, there was a nice fat official sign: Guthrie Turlock Donaldson, and over their names a trade sign with GTD embossed. So much for checking him out. She began to really feel good.

In the next few days, Sylvie went to Ensenada with Rob for the day; they went to L.A. and toured the studios there; they stopped at Disneyland. It was late at night, and she didn't want him to drive back, so they checked in at a warm, bright, clean motel. Without asking, Rob booked separate rooms for them. She would not have objected if they'd stayed in one room, maybe in separate beds; she wasn't quite sure yet how ready she was for anything more. So they slept in separate rooms. She was having a good time, and she tried not to think about how quickly the days were passing before she'd have to go back to work. Maybe she could see him occasionally, but nothing heavy like this. She decided, as she fell asleep in a strange room in Anaheim, thinking of him breathing and thinking of her just a wall's thickness away, that she must speak with him about that before things went any further.

The opportunity presented itself the next day. They were on that wonderful lawn, lying on deck chairs. He wore only his black swim trunks and looked wonderful to her. She wore a mauve bikini that showed off her smooth skin, her long legs, her small but shapely breasts. By now, she was no longer shy with him. He glowed with sun oil as he lay on his back, chin up, hands by his sides. His sunglasses made him seem machine-like. "Rob?"

"Mm?" He barely moved.

"Do you always have this much time on your hands?"

"Rarely." One hand fiddled with the sunglasses, and he stiffened a bit, apparently anticipating personal questions.

"I'm going to be really busy starting in about ten days. I just want you realize that."

"I'm sorry to hear that, but if that's the nature of your job——."

"Nothing personal. I'm having a really wonderful time and, well, I just thought you should know." She wondered if he could read into that her concern that, at this point, she was just having a fling, and she hoped it was that for him too. She wasn't ready to really open up to him in a serious way; she was puzzled about her behavior, since she was normally quite reserved and did not play around much. Since she couldn't explain this fling thing to herself, she didn't want to bring it up in conversation with him. Maybe, she thought, I just work too hard and want to blow off some steam. Can I blame myself for that?

"I'm going to be traveling again soon," he raising his glasses and regarding her with sincere hazel eyes. "I was concerned that perhaps——."

She rose and sat by his side. He reached up to touch her shoulders. She bent over him and kissed him hungrily. His tongue responded slowly to hers, as if tongues could be surprised. He clasped her hungrily to her, and finally she did feel his hands roving down her flanks, cupping her buttocks and letting go, over and over, then running along the smooth ramp of her waist. They went into the house, not bothering to close the back door, and rolled together on the thick rug. One by one, they peeled each other's clothes away, still locked in a steamy kiss that went on forever, it seemed. She felt his hardness against her, and touched herself. At the feeling of her own wetness, she felt herself moaning with desire. His small, precise hands found their way quickly to the right place. While he flicked her nipple with his tongue, alternating from one breast to the other, he found the track that ran around her own hardness, and she found herself pulsating inwardly. Spread-eagled, she felt too weak to do more than loosely embrace his magnificently skilled body. What he did to her breasts and down below sent her ever higher, moaning, arching her back, begging him, "yes! Yes! Yes!" When she climaxed, she felt an explosion that released months of frustration. Her image was that she lay straddling the sea, face up, and a volcano was blowing her into the sky.

She lay panting in his arms for a minute or two. He was still breathing hard, eyes still wild and unspent. "Here," she said, "let me." She pushed him onto his back and crawled down to where she could take him into her mouth. He began to moan.

They made love much of the afternoon and into the evening. By then they were hungry, and tired. They slipped into casual clothes and went to an Italian ristorante, where he feted her with an exotic pasta and dark red wine. Later they walked arm in arm along Nautilus and Pearl and various La Jolla side streets. They peered into the expensively arrayed show windows of a bookstore and a Persian carpet store and an antique dealer's, until they grew tired of looking at expensive baubles. They held hands and kissed often, like teenagers, as they strolled back to his car for the ride back to his house.

"That was a lot of fun," she said.

"It's been a wonderful day. Want to spend the night?"

"I'd love to, Rob." She leaned her head against his shoulder. She allowed herself to feel a liberating bliss, no matter what would happen when she started her next job or when he flew out of town or whatever.

In the living room, with that wonderful view of the sea, they clinked wine glasses. Rob excused himself and went to the bathroom.

The phone rang. And rang again. And rang a third time. Sylvie felt conflicting urges – to be civil and pick up, and to respect Rob's privacy and let it go. She looked around, but the bathroom door was closed, and she didn't know if she should call him. Might be nothing more than a wrong number.

"Matthew," a woman's voice said breathlessly. "Honey, I'm sorry. Are you back? I'm sorry we had a silly argument. I was hoping you'd gone back home, but I guess you must have gone on to Vegas. I'll pick up a few things and call you. Love you. Bye."

Rob came out, wiping his hands with a towel.

"Rob, who's Matthew?"

Rob's face underwent a strange little transition from questioning to smiling reassuringly, but along the way it passed through a dark zone for a fraction of a second that set off a faint thrill of alarm. She stilled it as soon as she felt it. "The phone rang and the message device went off," she added lamely to her question.

"Matthew is my brother. We haven't spoken in some time. What did he want?"

"It wasn't him, actually, but his wife or his girlfriend or something."

"I see." Rob got that dark something again in his eyes as he leaned across the couch and listened as he played the message back. "That was Neila," he said when the message was done. "Matthew's wife. They must have had a spat, and she thought he was staying with me."

"Of course," Sylvie said. She raised her glass in a toast, and he clinked his against hers. Still, something was a little different about him, somehow.

They sat out on the lawn for a while, under the stars. Rob had opened a good bottle of sweet asti spumante. They drank it chilled, from a cooler. Rob made small talk. "Do you know how champagne glasses got their shape? Supposedly, at the court of Louis XIV, they decided to honor Marie Antoinette by creating a new type of glass for their table. So they took an impression of one of her breasts while she leaned forward, and that's how it got that nice symmetrical and rather sexy shape."

Sylvie yawned. "That's nice, Rob. What a wonderful story."

Rob went on talking, and pretty soon Sylvie found herself dead tired. She couldn't move her hands anymore, nor could she even speak to ask him for a blanket.

In the morning, she awoke as a slat of sunshine guillotined through a curtain and threatened to split her head in half. She must have cried out in pain, for, minutes later, Rob entered carrying a tray. "Good morning!"

"Oh my God, my head hurts."

"You mixed wine and champagne, my darling. I should have known better. Here, as an apology, I've made a nice breakfast for you. And I have some aspirin."

She forced the aspirin tablets between her parched lips, and then drank from a glass of cool water. Rob gave her a salty broth that made her sweat, but restored much of her vitality. "God, I can't remember ever having a reaction like that to wine."

"Wine and champagne. We had red wine with dinner, white wine when we got here, and champagne out on the lawn. Do you remember dancing in the nude?"

"No!" She felt mortified.

He grinned mildly. "Darling, you were incredible. It was a better show than at the Purple Pony. Have you thought of working as a stripper?" He nuzzled his lips through her hair.

She couldn't eat the scrambled eggs, but she crunched on bacon and dry toast. Her stomach wasn't too bad, after all, and her hangover was lessening. She simply felt lousy and out of place and all she wanted to do now was to be home. She felt so embarrassed.

"Was I – noisy?"

"You mean while dancing? No, you were silent and mysterious."

"Good. At least I assume none of your neighbors saw me."

"Nobody can see us here. It's just you and me, darling."

"I need to go home and recuperate."

"Will I see you later today?"

She gave him a wan smile. "I'll call you later and let you know how I feel."

Later that morning, when she walked into her condo, she screamed. Someone had gone through the place. Books lay scattered on the floor amid papers and food and broken glass. She felt sick to her soul and started to cry as she staggered from one item of destruction to the next. The bed had been stripped, the mattress torn, the cushions thrown off the couch.

The police arrived within twenty minutes in the form of a man in a woolly herringbone business suit. A tired looking middle-aged man, with gray hair and sallow skin, introduced himself as Detective Sergeant David Amal. He showed her his badge and an I.D. card where his name was correctly spelled. "What happened?"

She spread her arms helplessly, started to explain the obvious, and started crying again. After a few minutes, she sat on the couch holding a tissue box on her lap, and he sat in a reconstructed easy chair opposite. "I don't know what happened. Maybe it was just a burglar."

Amal raised on eyebrow. "A burglar who was looking for something specific. A casual burglar would have grabbed your pc or your tv or your stereo" – he pointed to each item in turn – "and would have been out of here in a few minutes. We see that every day. This is different. So, Miss Bancroft, what was our burglar looking for?"

She reacted in horror. "My check! I just received a huge paycheck. If someone knew about that... but I just deposited it in the bank. But I had it here for a few days."

"Interesting. Maybe someone knows you hold on to checks, but didn't know you'd already deposited it. Someone connected with your employer?"

Sylvie frowned. Claire? No, how could someone so pleasant be responsible for a mess like this. Then again, what if she had an accomplice.

The phone rang. Amal got up to look around, holding his pen in one hand and a small pocket notebook in the other.

It was Rob. "Hi, just called to see how you are feeling."

"Terrible," she wailed and started crying again, "someone broke into my condo and trashed the whole place."

"I'm sorry to hear that. Can I come over and help?"

"Let me call you back a little later."

"Okay, darling. I'll be out, but I have my pager. You know the number."

"Yes. Thank you."

Frankly, she was suspicious of him too. He'd forced himself into her life, and within less than a week, this had happened.

As if to underscore her dismal feelings, a huge cloud bank was moving in from the Pacific. She cleaned off the small plastic radio from the kitchen and replaced it on its shelf. She comforted herself with music from her favorite radio station. Amal had apparently finished his inventory, for he said: "Well, Miss Bancroft, I see no unusual signs. The burglar, let's call him, forced the screen door on your patio. Simple. He – it was probably a man – came in and trashed the place. Who do you know that would come in looking for something specific? And what do you have they could be after?"

Within an hour, they had it narrowed down to Claire, or someone at the agency, or possibly someone from the company she'd just worked at for three months, or Rob. She was embarrassed about Rob. "Did this new boyfriend of yours know you held a large check?"

"No, I know I never told him."

"What if someone in the company you worked for knew? You say the agency sent the check ahead to save you a trip."

"Yes." A whole new world of suspicion dawned on her. She ran through, one by one, the people she'd worked with, while Amal took notes. "Susan Burman; she was kind of bitchy at times... Roger Lovell; tried to hit on me, kind of sleazy... Tim Barnes; stuffed shirt; never said a word to me... Rosa Goldbaum; nice girl; very bright; too small to force her way in..." She laughed at the thought of little Rosa scaling the drainpipe to the second floor and than shouldering her way through a locked aluminum bug door.

In the end, she could think of no person in particular who might have done this to her. Detective

Amal rose and shook her hand. "Unfortunately, we
are busy with some very serious cases and this
becomes an issue between you, the home owners'
association, and your insurance company. I wish you
the best, Miss Bancroft. Oh, and one other thing. You
should go through all your possessions and see if
anything is missing. If nothing is missing, give me
another call, because that would be very strange
indeed.

Sylvie spent hours cleaning, and gradually her
home began to look like itself again. The home
owners' president came over with an insurance
person, and they took notes and photos and reminded
her there was a $500 deductible on theft, in case she
found anything missing. Two workmen came and
installed new dead-bolts. They replaced the broken
screen door with a heavy duty steel security door.
They also hooked up a burglar detection kit that
would go off loudly if a window were broken. The
insurance company was paying, so Sylvie was at least
happy about that. She whistled as she put her twelve
roses back in a vase with fresh water.

The sun went down, the trash can overflowed, the
condo smelled of cleansers, and Sylvie stepped
tiredly into the shower. Soaping herself in the
comforting hot water, she remembered Detective
Amal's suggestion. Honestly, she had not noticed
anything missing.

After her shower, she dressed lightly, in shorts and
a t-shirt. She slipped shower clogs on in case there
was any broken glass left, though she'd swept,

mopped, and waxed thoroughly. The phone rang as she went into the kitchen. It was Rob. "Hi, honey, I didn't hear from you and I was worried."

"I'm okay now," she said. "Maybe it was just a prank by some teenagers, though I really can't quite believe it."

"Would you like me to spend the night with you there? So you feel safe?"

She puckered her mouth and thought. "Actually, I have a better idea. Why don't I come over to your place and spend the night?"

"I'd love that. Want me to pick you up?"

And not have her car? She thought about that for a moment. "You know, after all that I've been through today, and all the work I've had to do cleaning up, and as tired as I am, you know what? Yes. I deserve to feel totally helpless, dependent, and cared for, even if it's for one night."

"Want to go out to eat?"

"I'm just going to heat some soup. Want some?"

"Eh—I'll pick something up along the way."

"No wine for me. No champagne. Nothing."

"We'll drink imported spring water and I'll pick up some crackers and cheese."

"Deal." They exchanged kissing noises and hung up.

Sylvie hummed to herself and warmed up a can of soup. Cheese sounded good. She took her small block of smoked cheddar from the refrigerator and put it on the counter. She took down the box of crackers from the cupboard. Finally she reached for her favorite, extra-large carving knife in the wooden block by the sink.

Empty. She peered at the block, counting her knives. They were all there except the biggest one. For a moment, she remembered Amal's statement. Then she thought—nobody is going to burglarize my condo, leave my pc and all the other things, but take a battered old knife.

Rob arrived shortly thereafter. He kissed her passionately in the hallway. As she returned his kiss, she put her arms up around the back of his neck, and there she felt something raspy. She pulled her hand away and there was blood on it. "Ick!" she said. "What have you done to yourself?"

"Oh that," he said sheepishly, dabbing his neck with a tissue, "I was working on the sprinkler system in the yard. Little at a time, you know. I bent down, and when I rose up, I caught myself on a thorn bush. Nasty old thing."

"I'll clean it up for you." She started for the bathroom to get the first aid kit.

"Don't bother, it's nothing."

"No really."

"If you insist." So he sat patiently while she dabbed at the crust that had formed. She dabbed with hot water until it had dissolved. Then she cleaned out the wound and applied an adhesive bandage. "That's an odd looking wound," she said.

"It's an odd looking rose bush." They both laughed.

As he drove her to his house, he reached over several times and toyed with her hair or laid his hand on her leg. She twisted around so she could lean against his shoulder, hard to do with bucket seats, but she managed to lean her forearm on the back of his seat so her hand rested on his shoulder.

He parked inside the garage and they walked up into the house. "How about a midnight swim?" Rob asked, pinching her behind.

She pinched him back. "Sounds like a wonderful idea. I didn't bring my—oh, no, you don't mean—?"

"Birthday suits only," he said, lifting her t-shirt from behind.

Minutes later they were out on the lawn. She was naked except for a large beach towel that was thick and warm. The moon was still almost full, and the scene was as beautiful as ever. "Hang on a minute," Rob said. "I have to find the main switch for the pool lights."

"I don't want lights!"

"Don't worry. Nobody can see us."

She worried about it anyway, crinkling her toes in the cool grass.

"Ow! Damn!" he shouted.

She squealed as cold water sprinkled her bare shoulders.

"Ow God damn!"

"What did you do!" She couldn't see him in the shadows.

"I must have hit the sprinklers instead."

"Eeee! turn them off!" Sylvie hopped toward the house door to get away from the lawn. As she did so, she tripped and fell. For a second she fell through empty space. Then she landed on her back, stunned. The hole he was digging—she'd fallen into it. Luckily the earth was fresh and soft at the bottom, about three feet down. Something smelled awful down here.

His shadow blotted out the moon above. "Oh my God. Are you hurt?"

She coughed and tried to sit up. "I'll tell you in a moment."

"Sylvie, darling, take my hand." He took both her hands and pulled her up.

"Whew, something stinks down there."

"There is an old septic line here, from before the sewer days. I'm so sorry, darling, let me kiss you. Come, it's just a little dirt, let's take a quick shower and then dive in."

They showered together, soaping each other. He examined her back and found no cuts or bruises. She examined his scratch and found it to look clean. "I'll have to bandage you again after our swim."

"C'mon!" He tapped her lightly on the behind and ran to the pool. He dove in and she followed. They described two nearly parallel arcs of bubbles in the aqua water. The pool was lit inside, so the water glowed. The water felt warm, but the air seemed fresh. They dove in a few more times, then huddled together for warmth by the diving board.

"It's so wonderful here," she said. "Look at the stars!"

A jet flew by overhead, and Rob said: "Sometimes when I'm on a night flight to L.A., I can look down as the plane takes off, and see all these swimming pools up the coast. Maybe the passengers are all leaning to one side to see you naked."

"Let them."

The swim tired her. They made love again, this time upstairs in the master bedroom. They fell asleep, spooning.

In the middle of the night, a sound woke her up. She was alone and the bed was cold. It took her a moment or two to realize where she was. Where was Rob?

She heard a repetitive sound, like coins being dropped one by one into a bag in another room. The sound was muffled.

She rose to visit the bathroom briefly, intending to slip back into the bed and go right back to sleep. The sound was louder here, and she lifted the roll-down window shade by the toilet seat.

Now she heard the sound more clearly.

The window afforded a view down through some vines overlooking the back lawn. She saw the swimming pool, the deck chairs, everything clearly in the moonlight. The sound was that of a shovel. The wielder of the shovel was Rob, standing in the hole where she'd fallen. And lying on the lawn beside the hole was a long shape draped in what looked like an old nylon sail.

Her breath froze in her throat with a tiny squeak. There was clearly something wrong here. Suddenly some scary ideas fell into place for her, and she realized she must get out of her. To be on her own turf. To think things through.

Quickly, she padded into the bedroom and found her clothes. Jeans, shirt, shoes... Her hands were shaking so badly she couldn't get her socks on. Forget them. She grabbed her sweater off the back of a chair and stopped to listen.

For a moment or two the blood pounded so hard in her throat that she couldn't hear.

No, the sound of the shovel had stopped.

Was he coming up the stairs?

She ran back into the bathroom and looked out the window. Rob and the shape were gone. But she had not dreamed this—the shovel stood in the hole, which was now a good two feet deeper. Maybe this was just crazy, she thought, of course it was just crazy, but she was too terrified to take a chance. She hardly knew this man, and here she was carrying on a torrid affair with him, and now she realized she was probably in over her head.

She took her shoes off and tiptoed across the bedroom.

Gingerly, she turned the door handle.

It made a soft squealing sound that reverberated through the dark, and she felt beads of sweat mix with tears in the orbs of her eyes.

There was nothing now but go for it. She pulled the door open, slowly, softly, listening.

Nothing. Just the ticking of a clock.

She slipped out into the hallway. Luckily it was carpeted. Her feet were soundless on the thick pile rug.

Moonlight seeped throughout the house, illumining the pictures of innocent family members—clean-cut boys and girls, happy women, smiling men—on the walls around her.

She ducked into one doorway and was prepared to run a few more feet to the next doorway, when something came up out of the yawning darkness of the steps leading downstairs.

She nearly fell over backwards and stood teetering in the darkness of an open bedroom as Rob walked past.

If he could not hear her on the rug, she could not hear him either. He moved like a ghost in the darkness.

In his hand was her missing kitchen knife. Its blade was long enough to slice all the way through her body. Its blade was wide and heavy and could double as a chopper. He held it like a sword as he passed by. She could smell the loam, the sweat, and the fresh air mixed in his hair. His mouth was half open, as if he were hungry. His face was radiant in moonlight, and his eyes shone with the radiance of an eerie trance.

She nearly screamed.

He walked past, leaving a wake of earthy smells.

In seconds, he would be in the bedroom.

She walked one, two, three, four, five, six big steps and turned left. A fleeting, terrified glance told her he was in the bedroom and had not seen her. She fled down the stairs with bolting feet, making more noise than she'd wanted to; across the living room, through the front hall, and out into the free fresh air of the driveway.

Terror propelled her along, running at top speed. Halfway to the street she remembered she was still holding her shoes. She knelt down to put them on.

That saved her life. For the moment.

She was hidden from sight by a round juniper bush.

Rob ran past her like an athlete, barely breathing hard, and waving the knife. He was wiry, and light on his feet.

She crouched as low as she could. The bush was only about three feet high and two feet across. She couldn't hide in it, and it would only conceal her as long as she stayed on the side opposite from him. The trick was now—where was he? She must see him first, or he'd soon find her.

Then she spotted him. He stood on the corner above, looking casual as he waited. The devil! He knew that, if she'd gotten off the grounds, he'd hear her. He didn't hear her, so he was waiting. There was no way she could get past that vantage point. He had her trapped. She examined her options. She must crawl backwards from bush to bush, as silently as possible—oh but how the grass swished! The sound wound through the still air of this evil night as if looking for him, to wrap itself around his neck and whisper leeringly in his ear where she was, where he would find her.

She crawled, banging her elbows on stray stones, weepy with pain, dirty and sweaty and terrified.

Her path took her into the deepening shade of a large willow tree. If she rose, he could see her profile against the mild light from the picture windows. She could try to scale the wall to get to the neighbors— but the bushes would be noisy. He'd be down here slicing at her before she could get up the wall.

Only one thing to do.

Crouching low, she ran through the grass along the edge of the driveway. When she got close to the house, she accidentally kicked a pebble, and it slapped against the wood door. No matter now; she ran into the house, closed the door, and bolted it.

In the fireplace, she found a hefty brass poker resembling a small harpoon. With that in hand, she found a phone and dialed 911.

"Emergency. How can I help you."

"A man is trying to kill me." She was breathless, and she had to whisper, for any moment he would be at the door.

The voice sounded bored, and the woman was chewing gum. "Are you in a residence or public building?"

"A house. A home. It's—his home. He has a knife."

"Are you in a safe spot?"

"I'm in the house. I've locked him out."

"What is the address?"

"I—I don't know." She couldn't remember. "Number 2995 something up in La Jolla. Off of Scenic Drive. One of these damn millions of dead end streets."

"Just a moment, we are tracing your call."

The line went dead.

"Oh Jesus. Hello? Hello?" She dropped the phone.

One of the windows exploded inward in a shower of glass. A heavy garden chair, white and wrought-iron, came crashing into the living room. It rolled, bouncing, and came to rest against the couch. Glass bits stung her cheeks.

Sylvie raised the poker and ran toward the bulging curtains where Rob was just backing in. He had one foot over the windowsill and he switched the knife to the hand closer to her, when she hit him full across the back. She slipped and fell. The poker fell clattering on the floor. Rob lay cringing in pain, but he still had the knife.

Sylvie jumped up and ran toward the back door, which was still open.

She heard him behind her.

As she ran across the lawn, she felt his hand grasping her sweater. As he slowed her to a stop, she screamed. At that moment, she tripped again and fell into the hole. Rob crashed in behind her. It stank in here. She saw the knife flying through the air, knocked from his grasp as he fell over her, past her. For a moment he looked stunned. She tried to stand up, but he pulled her down with one hand while fumbling for the knife with the other. She reached out blindly and felt something against her fingertips. The handle of the shovel. She lurched toward it.

As he pulled her toward him again, the handle was in her hand. She yanked the handle toward Rob in a fast arc, striking him full in the face. As his nose erupted in a fountain of blood, she raised the shovel up and hit him over the head.

Without looking back, and without taking time or breath to scream anymore, she ran through the house and into the street. There were no keys in the Porsche. She was afraid to ever set foot in the house again, so she started running.

She was far from any help. There were darkened and shuttered houses on either side of the long street, but she was too terrified to stop and bang on doors. It must be three or four in the morning. If she made enough noise, she might wake somebody, but by then Rob would find her. God, she hadn't realized that it must be several miles to the nearest gas station, much less one that was open at this hour.

The streets floated by one by one as she jogged. There was an insular, fortified sameness about the houses. They were big, upper middle-class, many with horseshoe driveways, many with interesting carriage lamps. Every once in a while, a sound-activated light would switch on.

She heard a sound behind her. The Porsche.

She ducked behind some parked cars and peered between the fenders as the familiar car purred past. He was looking for her, it was clear. Going about 30 miles an hour, carefully scanning right and left. He held a cloth to his nose. His eyes were black and frightening in the night light. He speeded up and rounded a corner with squealing tires. He was angry and his car said so.

Sylvie spotted a loose padlock on a garage door. She sprinted down the driveway, lifted the door a foot or two, slid underneath, and prayed that there was no dog in the house. There wasn't. She emptied a bin of laundry and made herself a nest in a corner. She did not sleep a wink all night but sat in the corner shivering, listening for him to come. He didn't.

In the morning, Sylvie crawled out of the garage, and knocked on doors until she was taken inside by an elderly couple who fed her breakfast and called the police for her. Detective Amal had a few surprises for her when he arrived. He drove an unmarked car, no Porsche by any means, but Sylvie felt safe. She almost wanted to hug him.

Then she froze in alarm. "Why are we driving this way?" They were headed back to Rob's house.

"Don't worry. We have several policemen there. Ever hear the names Matthew and Neila Tinsley?"

She remembered the answering device. "There was a Matthew..."

"Yes, well, he came to see our Missing Persons office about his wife Neila. It turns out that Matthew and Neila Tinsley are the legal owners and long-time inhabitants of the house you thought was owned by this Rob Turlock. Dr. Matthew Tinsley is a psychiatrist at UCSD Medical Center in Hillcrest. Dr. Neila Tinsley is a Professor of Linguistics at UCSD in LaJolla. They had scheduled a two-week vacation to Las Vegas and other points. On the day they were due to leave, they had a big argument. She flew to her parents' house in New Orleans while Matthew continued on along the scheduled vacation path. Both began to feel sorry about their behavior, but neither was quite ready to call the other. According to the airline offices, Neila flew back to San Diego the night you mentioned the call—."

"—Which is on the recording device—."

"—No. Our friend Turlock is quite clever, and very thorough. The tape's been yanked out and probably thrown someplace where we'll never find it, although we'll keep looking for it. I think Turlock knew somehow that these people were going to be away on vacation. I think he was just having a grand old time showing off this place, which wasn't his at all. What bothers me is that he tried to kill you. Given that, I'm very worried about Neila Tinsley because she dropped in unexpectedly and must have upset his plans."

They arrived at the house, which was sealed off with yellow police tape. Several police cars stood parked on the block, and a throng of neighbors stood gawking. Sylvie walked with Amal toward the house. She described how she'd hid in the bushes as Rob ran by with the knife, and the thought of it made her want to go to pieces. She felt somehow strong now, having held her own. With the police on her side, she felt a return of normalcy.

Among the various police in the house, uniformed and plainclothes, it was easy to see who was Matthew Tinsley. He was a fiftyish, graying man, slim, looked nothing at all like Rob or Rob's brother, and his eyes were filled with tears. Amal introduced Sylvie, and for a moment Sylvie thought Matthew was going to hit her. She said: "I'm sorry. I didn't know I was violating the privacy of your house. He violated me in more ways than one."

Surprisingly, Matthew seemed understanding. "Don't worry about the house. I'm just worried that something happened to my wife."

"These are all your family members?" Sylvie asked, looking at the photos that covered every piece of furniture in the living room, except those thrown over and covered with broken glass from the fight last night.

"Yes. Here's Neila." He pointed to a photo of an attractive, smiling blonde woman in her thirties. "Twenty years ago."

Sylvie shook her head in amazement, thinking of how Rob had completely wrapped her in his conspiracy. The sprinklers, she thought, and told Amal: "He told me the hole in the yard was for the sprinklers, because they were old and not working anymore. Then he accidentally turned them on, and they work perfectly. I was drenched."

They walked outside, where several men and women clustered around the hole. They watched as a police woman led a dog around the lawn and into the hole. Amal told Sylvie, softly, to spare the feelings of Matthew, who stood anxiously wringing his hands and wiping tears away: "The dog is especially trained to sniff out human corpses. It's not a service we advertise much, because it sounds kind of grisly."

"Nothing here," the police woman said, climbing out of the hole. She dusted off her pants and whistled for the dog to climb up. "Smells like a dead mouse or something. The dog sniffed around, but didn't get excited. There is nothing in this hole."

Sylvie told Amal quietly: "But I saw a nylon sail or something. It had to have a body inside. It was that kind of lump." Then she slapped her forehead. "Of course! After Neila called, he got me drunk. No, I think he drugged me to put me to sleep. The call alarmed him, and he suddenly had to have me out of his hair for the night. And the scratches on the back of his neck. I'll bet he did something to Neila when she showed up, and she managed to scratch him. I thought those were funny looking scratches for a rose bush."

Amal nodded slowly. "A horrible story, but it seems to hang together. There are still lots of loose ends, of course. Most notably, we are on the lookout for Rob Turlock, but nobody has seen him yet. A matter of time, I suppose, but I hope he can't hurt anyone else before he's caught."

Sylvie held her head, reeling at the events she'd gone through. Suddenly, working 14 hours a day 7 days a week seemed like a safer, saner way to live.

A uniformed officer approached. "Sarge, wanna see what we found down the street?"

"Sure." Sylvie, Amal, and the officer walked some distance down the street to where a couple of cops were hauling the tarp off the back of an old, battered green pickup truck. Its cargo area was filled to the brim with soil and clods of grass. The dog handler was there, and the German shepherd jumped up with tail wagging. The dog sniffed eagerly.

Sylvie's stomach turned. Matthew Tinsley ran toward the truck with a shout of anguish and disbelief.

But the dog jumped down with a demure whimper, and the police woman shook her head. "Nothing."

Matthew Tinsley cried with relief. Sylvie wanted to put her arm around him to comfort him, but she felt terribly tainted. She wasn't sure he wanted to be comforted by a woman who'd had sex with a monster. Tears ran down her cheeks at the thought. She must find some way to cleanse herself, but how? The thought of his hands on her began to make her feel like wilting.

"Just soil," the policemen said. "No bodies or anything. Just a truck full of soil."

"Soil," Sergeant Amal repeated. "I want this soil analyzed, but I think we'll find it's the soil from the hole in back."

"Dr. Tinsley, did you have a project going to repair your sprinklers?"

"That's goddam ridiculous. I just paid thousands for a complete new sprinkler system last year."

"Rob Turlock lied to you about that, Miss Bancroft. It seems evident he is responsible for the hole. If so, what was the purpose of it?"

She remembered him helping her up when she'd fallen into it, and shuddered. "I guess he meant to bury someone in it."

"But not – forgive me, Dr. Tinsley – Neila. Let's see. Somehow, a lot of planning went into this. He went to a lot of trouble. So he must have had a specific use for the hole. Neila wasn't on his schedule, because her arrival would have been unplanned. That leaves you, Miss Bancroft."

"Oh thanks a million."

"You are a very lucky woman."

A policeman approached holding a cell phone. "We ran a make on this truck. Belongs to Malpeth Landscaping in Mira Mesa. Want me to patch you through to Mr. Malpeth, the owner?"

"Sure." Amal took the cell phone and walked off to one side. He paced up and down nodding, conversing, occasionally slapping his forehead. When he was done, he put the cell phone in his pocket and told the uniformed officer in charge: "Malpeth says he's done jobs like this for a Mr. Gascoigne, who fits the description of Rob Turlock. We can probably assume that Turlock is an alias, and that Gascoigne is also. Can you see if you track down this Gascoigne lead?"

"Sure," the officer said.

"Dr. Tinsley, there is nothing you can do to help right now. One of the officers will go with you to the house and maybe you could stand by—?"

Tinsley seemed angry, which was to be expected, Sylvie thought, but equally heartbroken and helpless. He let himself be led gently by two policemen.

Amal spoke to Sylvie and several policemen. "Mr. Malpeth is going to fax us a list of jobs he's done for Gascoigne. He says there have been about seven or eight. I didn't want Tinsley to hear about this. I suspect we have a serial killer on our hands. Miss Bancroft, if you have time, would you mind tagging along? I have a few things to check out, and I'd feel better about your safety."

"Oh what fun. Yes, I have another week off, and I have nothing better to do."

Amal ordered his associates: "I want a city crew to stand by in case we need to dig. I want a judge on standby to issue warrants, writs, whatever we need to go on private property."

While they waited for the fax, Amal and Sylvie drove down to central La Jolla. As Amal parked the car, Sylvie found that her hands were trembling. He said: "You don't have to go through with this if you don't want to."

Her teeth chattered, but she said: "I have to. I feel so dirty inside, and I want this bastard caught."

"I understand. You are a brave woman."

They walked along the sunny street, where art galleries dozed in the shade of pine trees. They came to the GTD Building and entered. In the lobby, Amal showed his gold shield and requested to see Mr. Turlock. Sylvie's knees shook together while the receptionist went to get Turlock.

Two minutes later, out came a tall, puzzled, and very friendly Mr. Turlock. Sylvie gasped. Mr. Turlock was a heavyset Afro-American with very distinguished gray muttonchops. "How can I help you?" he asked extending a hand.

Sylvie and Amal shook Turlock's hand.

"You already have," Amal said. He handed Turlock the card "Rob" had given Sylvie. "Is this your card?"

"Yes."

"Any idea how it got into Ms. Bancroft's hands?"

Turlock studied her. "We've never met, have we, young lady?"

"Nossir, we haven't. Are you in finance? Stocks? Bonds?"

Turlock laughed. "We are a Real Estate Investment Trust management company. In that sense, we are."

Amal said: "Would this property mean anything to you?" He mentioned Tinsley's address.

"We'd have to research it. Come in, come in." Turlock – the real Rob Turlock – ushered them into a large sitting room furnished with plush leather easy chairs, couches, a pleasant atmosphere with potted palms and tall narrow windows. The drapes had earth colors and subdued fishes in a kind of hemp design, and the seahorses made Sylvie feel sick. Pregnancy test! She used the pill, but she must get tested. After a short while, Turlock came back: "No, I'm sorry, that property is owned by the Tinsleys, free and clear, and we have nothing to do with it."

Amal rose and said: "Just out of curiosity, Mr. Turlock, have you gone on vacation recently?"

"Why… about a year ago. Why?"

"Just wondering. How long were you gone?"

"I took my wife and kids to Bermuda for ten days."

"I may need to get in touch with you again."
"By all means."

After they left the GTD building, Sylvie excused herself for a moment. She went to a pharmacy to buy a pregnancy testing kit. There, she discovered she didn't have enough cash on hand. She stepped around the corner to an ATM machine, inserted her card and code, and waited. When the next menu slowly made its way to the screen, she entered a request for $60. The terminal displayed a warning: "Not enough money available to cover the requested amount."

"No!" She stepped back. "No! My money!" Her $15,000 that she'd worked so hard for, and which she needed to cover her mortgage, her expenses – it just couldn't be.

"What is it?" Amal said, coming to her aid after having waited at a respectful distance.

"We've got to go to my bank!"

"Hold on." He produced the cell phone. "Call them right now from here." Sylvie's fingers were so shaky he had to dial for her.

A Mrs. Pendergast answered, and Sylvie stammered out her problem. "So you are Mrs. Turlock?"

"No, I'm Sylvie Bancroft."

"Your husband did mention you go by your maiden name. Your money is here, safe and in one piece."

"Oh thank God." She sagged against the wall, knees bent, her back sliding slowly down until she was in a squatting position.

"Your husband—."

"I don't have a husband. He's a criminal."

"I'm sorry. Dear, dear, I'm so glad we take precautions. He walked in with a check in your name made out to him—."

"—What? —."

"—and requested we move your money to a joint account. He had the paperwork all filled in, including your signature."

"Oh my God."

"We have a rule that you'd have to sign in front of one of our officers after showing i.d. I tried calling you numerous times, but there was no answer." Mrs. Pendergast mentioned the number, and Sylvie was not surprised that it was the Tinsleys' phone number. This would be after "Rob" had thrown the tape away.

Sylvie fumbled in her purse. "What's the check number?" She pulled out her checkbook. Mrs. Pendergast said, "Number 2435." Sylvie leafed through her unsigned checks and sure enough, that number check was missing. "Thank you," she said and hung up.

Amal said: "I'll have to talk with her about this when there's time. I caught the drift of your conversation."

Sylvie rose. "He drugged me, probably killed Neila, and then drove to my condo and calmly rifled the whole place. And do you know what? The whole time, my checkbook was under the driver's side seat of my car, tucked under the carpet. I hid it there unconsciously, probably because I was a little uptight about this guy."

"Miss Bancroft, that may be true, but think. He took the knife. There was more than one purpose for his visit to your place."

"What do you mean?'

"It's still a little premature to say." The cell phone rang, and he answered. "Yes? Oh really. Good work. Okay. Just start at the bottom of the list. The most recent. Let's try and hit them all today." He put the phone away and started toward his car. "Come on, Miss Bancroft. We have the list, and we're going to the most recent property prior to the Tinsleys'."

As they drove back up into the La Jolla hills, Amal said: "Four La Jolla residences, two in Loma Portal, one in Fairbanks Ranch, one in Del Mar. Our man picks residences where the owners are on vacation. He sets up an attractive woman and convinces her he's Rob Turlock, a wealthy guy. He wines her, dines her, loves her – and kills her with a knife from her kitchen. Might be a ritual thing. Could be bipolar disorder, schizophrenia, hears voices, who knows what. I suspect he follows the same pattern each time. A methodical, precise individual."

Sylvie remembered Rob's small, neat fingers, and nearly retched.

They pulled up at a lavish ultra-modern house of white beams and steel sculptures. The sculptures were burnished and shone in the sun, but had rusty-looking jagged edges that inadvertently seemed designed for the ghoulish atmosphere. Several police cars stood in the driveway. There was a babble of voices, and two news vans arrived. Amal talked on the phone as he and Sylvie walked around the side of the house. "Brace yourself," he said.

A dense horseshoe of people surrounded a newly dug trench about the same dimensions as the one at the Tinsleys'. A small backhoe sat idle to one side while a crew of city workers dug carefully in the hole.

About three feet down, lying on its back, was the skeleton of a woman. A few whisps of leathery skin clung to her skull, and it was clear she'd had a full head of healthy black hair. Her eye sockets stared vacantly at the sky, and her teeth showed not a grin but a grimace. Her hands had been folded over her chest, and among the finger bones was a large butcher knife, pointed down toward her feet. The nameless victim had been buried in a wedding dress that lay carefully fanned out, as if "Rob" had taken great care to lay out his bride in style.

Sylvie cried out and turned away.

Later in the day, Amal called Sylvie at home to tell her the green Porsche (Matthew Tinsley's) had been found abandoned in Chula Vista, not far from the Mexican border. In the trunk was the body of Neila Tinsley. She'd been dead about three days and wrapped multiple times in a large plastic painter's tarp that kept in the smell of decomposition. "She wasn't part of his plan," Amal said. "He's a precise, methodical character and her arrival must have really knocked him for a loop. But he dealt with it efficiently − drugged you, killed her, disposed of her body, rifled your place. The plastic tarp you saw was probably meant for you, but he used it on her. And he probably had her body in the car when he came to pick you up that last night. I'm sorry. I thought you'd want all the facts."

Sylvie was too numb to feel shocked or scared or bad for herself any more. Poor Matthew, she thought, after Amal left, as she sipped coffee in her kitchen. Poor Neila. Poor brides, whoever they'd been. By evening, Amal's people had turned up seven of "Rob's brides in various back yards. Sylvie felt sick about the affair she'd had with the creep, but she felt even more nauseated at the thought that she might have wound up as one of those brides.

Amal stopped by to see her. She poured coffee for the two of them, and Amal held out a black object that she saw, when she looked at it closely, was a cassette. "Put it in your vcr," he urged.

They sipped coffee as they waited for the cassette to begin playing. She nearly dropped her coffee. There was footage of her on her patio, wearing only the Ensenada t-shirt and the torn old Bermudas. She was laughing, stripping off yellow gloves, as she spoke with him on the portable phone. "He said he had trouble finding the place," she said disgustedly. "He was stalking me all along. No wonder he always had my favorite radio station playing."

"Yes. He knew your habits. Your interests. You were a temporary worker with few friends, forgive me for being blunt. You might not be missed for a long time. If you didn't show up for a job, they'd assume you flaked out, and they'd hire someone else that very morning. Just think of this – we have no clue who our man is; but we also still don't know who half his victims were."

"Please keep protecting me."

"Don't worry. We have two uniformed policemen on the grounds, and a bunch of plainclothes people in the area. We really want to catch this guy, and protect you at the same time."

Sylvie asked: "Do you think he fled to Mexico?" She eyed the empty slot in her cutting board as she spoke; its emptiness reminded her of an emptiness she felt.

"It's possible." Amal paused. "However, we have to assume he might have doubled back. Don't forget, he dumped the Porsche three blocks from the trolley line. He could have ridden south to San Ysidro and crossed the border, but he could just as well be back in central San Diego already. We'll all have to keep up our guard."

Sylvie was exhausted, but she slept poorly that night. She was afraid to take a sleeping tablet for fear that He might sneak up on her. She realized it would take years for her to get over the mistake she'd made. As she tied up her garbage bag, she noted that it contained the last of the debris from her housewreck – including the red roses he'd given her. She threw the bag as far as she could into the big dumpster outside.

Next morning, her pregnancy test was negative, thank God. She checked into a specialized clinic at UCSD Medical Center that dealt with rape victims. She was tested for v.d. and declared clean. She met a counselor and scheduled weekly therapy sessions starting that morning. She cried a lot in the sunny room with the psychologist, an American woman of Pakistani extraction who was a good listener. The full horror of what had happened – and worse yet, what had nearly happened – to her was just becoming clear. She'd work through it, though; just having someone to talk to made her feel better.

Her shrink told her in her soft, lilting accented voice: "We will probably never get to know what he is like inside, even if he is captured. What I see is a man who both intensely loves and hates, probably also fears, women. The woman's knife represents to him her power that he fears and hates. He steals the knife from her. He ravishes her, overpowers her, weds her, and kills her. Then he buries her with the symbol of her power, the knife, aimed at the center of her sexuality, as if he had used her power to kill her and thereby momentarily liberate himself. Until the next cycle."

Amal called later in the day. "We still haven't cornered our man. We don't even know his name. But we've begun tying together some of the loose ends. It turns out that he tapped into the computer at a travel agency. That's how he picked the host families, if I may make the analogy to a virus or some sort of parasitic insect. Without the travel agency knowing, he threw in a package deal to watch the house and also bring in gardening and cleaning crews for a modest price, so they'd find their house sparkling when they returned. And people did find their house sparkling, with a new flower bed. What they didn't know was that the flower bed doubled as a cemetery. By the way, there is one buried in the real Mr. Turlock's flower garden. Our man was quite busy while the Turlocks were on vacation."

Sylvie began working for a new company in a few days. She immersed herself in her work. She estimated that she would produce about 15,000 lines of code over a four month period, earn over $20,000, and have a long vacation into January. She scrapped any plans to go to Cabo, and planned to visit her parents. While she worked, she often slept at the office, not so much to be close to her work, as to avoid going home. She began thinking of selling the condo, even though she might take a loss.

Amal still called regularly to check on her, and there was always a plainclothes police man or woman on the grounds to protect her and to catch her victimizer. She had a police-issue walkie-talkie in the kitchen in case the telephone failed and she had to call the police in a hurry; at the other end was always a cop in the yard. Amal said it was his favorite case now; his hobby; his passion. It was not unusual for him to visit her for a few moments in person once or twice a week, to putter around inspecting the grounds as if he expected to find new clues.

Therapy went well, although there seemed to be a wall beyond which her healing would not go. She couldn't even name the wall or explain it – she only knew that it was something traumatic that must be dismantled before she could be free, and neither she nor the shrink could figure out how that would be done.

By November, Sylvie realized that her temp job was almost done. She was beginning to work more normal hours, and she began to sleep at the condo regularly. She'd arranged with Amal that the plainclothes person would check in with her twice – once when she got home, and a second time around eleven, right before she went to bed. Even at that, she had trouble sleeping, and she often had terrible dreams, but she no longer felt as terrible. Slowly, she was healing.

A great rain storm pummeled California in the middle of November. San Diego felt the brunt as the edges of the storm pushed through the county. Traffic was backed up. People were hurt in accidents. Rain beat down in torrents. Sylvie hurried home as best she could, taking side streets. The gutters were bloated with black-looking water and floating trash. She was soaking wet when she entered her condo.

She took off her soggy coat and hung it on the peg in back of the door. She stood her dripping umbrella, open, on its edge on the hardwood floor behind the door. She smelled something a little odd, but dismissed it as having to do with the rain. A rich aroma of soil and flowers and wetness blew through the gloomy apartment, propelled by a fresh wind.

Every once in a while, she really liked a downpour. The sunny weather here was great, but downright boring at times. She stepped out of her damp clothing as she walked to the bathroom. There, she stripped off her undies and stepped into a hot, steamy shower. Afterward, humming, wearing only a large bath towel, she made herself coffee and put a frozen spaghetti dinner in the microwave.

And froze.

In the weak kitchen light, she saw clearly that the missing knife was back in its slot in the wooden block. She whirled, and immediately saw the cause of the odd smell she'd noticed earlier: someone had placed twelve dark-red roses in her favorite crystal vase.

She started for the kitchen, to call Amal. Her towel slipped down, and she remembered to go into her bedroom to put some jeans and a sweatshirt on. She saw a shadow in the closet and screamed; but it was only her long black dress. Trembling, more afraid even than she'd been right after her affair, she dialed the police.

Her phone was dead.

She went into the kitchen and spoke into the walkie talkie. Nothing. The battery must be dead.

She checked the doors and found them locked, especially the new steel security door overlooking the patio.

Lightning flashed, followed by thunder, and she thought she saw something out of the patio, but maybe it was just her hanging collection of epiphytes.

She huddled on the couch, trying to figure out what to do. Should she sit tight? Or make a run for it – get Amal? Her cop wasn't due for another hour. That was it – she'd wait an hour.

She kept the lights off and the electronics off – no radio, no tv, no computer. She waited. And she listened. She could almost hear the beating of her heart amid the patter of rain. Gusts of wind drove up against the windows, rising and ebbing with faint deep howling sounds. People were still at work, she thought, for the other condos seemed dark and deserted. She hardly dared go near any windows.

Suddenly, she started. There was a sound on the redwood patio deck. Was that a figure she saw fleeting through fog and night?

There was a thump on against the wall outside. That did it. Sylvie jumped up, put on her still-soggy rain coat, picked up her umbrella, and ran outside. She locked and bolted her door and ran down the carpeted hallways to find her police watcher.

Instead, she found a body. Sprawled against the wall, still in his coat, was Amal. His throat had been slit, and his tongue protruded slightly. His eyes were half open, as if he were just waking up from a sleep. His mouth seemed about to yawn. It wasn't unusual for him to check on her watchers, and to stop by to visit her. He'd rather liked her, though he was older and married, and she'd gotten to like him as a friend and protector. Right now, she was wired beyond reason. She fumbled in his clothing, looking for his gun – it was gone. He wore a pager on his belt, but no cell phone, no walkie-talkie – someone had taken it away! The person who'd killed him! She must run outside and find –

But at that moment she saw a shadow on the wall – large head, small precise fingers. The man who had raped her with his lies and murderous deceptions. She glimpsed his cold features, his big hungry eyes as he came up the stairs. "Sylvie," he said.

She screamed and ran back to her condo. She heard his running footsteps a few feet behind her on the hallway floor as she fumbled with her lock. She got the door open, slipped inside, and slammed it shut – at the same moment He collided with the door. He wasn't strong enough to push it in, though he kicked it violently and rapidly for a minute or so. How could he exert that much force for so long without breaking his foot, she wondered.

Nobody called out for him to stop. She was all alone.

Sylvie was alone. He had a gun and he meant to kill her. She wasn't strong enough to resist his wiry strength.

She ran into the kitchen and took from the wooden block the very butcher knife he planned to bury with her corpse. She ran through the condo flicking off light switches. She had no doubt he'd get in somehow—but perhaps she could ambush him in the dark. Strange, she thought, how she wasn't crying or sobbing or hysterical. I'm beyond that, she thought. I will be dead soon. If I can just take him with me, then I will be clean. She remembered the scratches on the back of his neck, and wondered if Neila Tinsley had had the same thought.

Sylvie sat against the back wall of the condo, in her living room, with the knife in both hands between her thighs, and waited.

Then the kicking began. He must be raging insane, she thought, feeling his kicks in her back as the wall shook. The wooden door slid open, letting in a draft of cool night-scented air with a hint of jasmin. What a lovely fragrance to die by, she thought, gripping the knife, knowing their final meeting was minutes away.

The kicking stopped.

She frowned, listening.

She heard the snap of a safety. He was going to shoot the lock off the steel door.

She reached behind her for something to lean against, felt instead the light cord, heard the big ceramic light stand fall off her letter-writing table and crash to the ground.

He fired the first shot. The metal whined as the bullet bounced off and then tore along the florentined steel, no doubt leaving a furrow. That was a police gun, a heavy piece, probably a 9 millimeter. She'd read about those. They could stop a maniac at a safe distance. Think what it would do to her door.

He fired another shot.

"Sylvie!"

She pulled the broken lamp toward her.

"I love you!"

He fired again, and the door jumped in its frame. The lock was still intact, but the tremendous force was tearing the door out of the wall.

"Sylvie!"

He rattled the door, and it gave with a wild groan.

She unplugged the lamp.

He fired again. The wall shook as the door bucked.

She tore the cord out of the broken lamp.

He fired again, and then shoved with all his might. Bits of torn wood and drywall few through the air. She saw him on the door, trying to bring it crashing down into the living room under his weight.

His body blocked out the dim light from outside.

She plugged in the cord.

He jumped up and down, shooting into the air until the gun was empty. He threw the gun aside and began a final onslaught to bring the door down and land in her living room.

The door was wet, and his manic gyrations sent sprays of water through the living room. The door crashed down, smashing the glass in her coffee table.

Sylvie touched the bare wires, where they'd been connected inside the lamp, to the wet metal door. There was a loud bang and a smell of burned flesh. The nameless man screamed.

The shock blew Sylvie back. She ignored the pain in her hands and crawled back to the door. "No!" he screamed hoarsely. His eyes were red, and his mouth frothed with blood. He held up his two charred hands imploringly—they were on fire, burning with flickering tongues of flame—and cried out in a voice thickened and almost bubbling with blood: "No! Please, Sylvie, I love you!"

She touched the cord to the door, and his expression deepened into one of great concentration. He seemed to arch his back while he gripped some invisible hold before him on the door more tightly with his burned claws. Smoke rose from the back of his collar, and suddenly he collapsed. Sylvie realized the fuse must have blown, because the cord in her hand was no longer live with electricity. She cried out in pain, for liquid copper had spilled on her hands and knees from the melting wires.

She heard running feet. People came to see about the shooting. Hugging her burned hands painfully to her belly, Sylvie rose on shaky legs. It was over. A small fire burned on the back of his jacket, and she let it. She wanted it to burn all the way into that empty hole where his soul should have been.

Funny thing, she thought as paramedics bandaged her hands and led her to a police car for a ride through the rain with sirens flashing. Funny thing – now she'd never know his real name. And, she reflected, that was probably for the best. She felt clean inside, for the first time since all this had begun. She would never know his name, and that was good, because it would be as if he had never existed. And she knew, as the passing streetlights flashed alternate bars of light and darkness over her lap, that sometimes she would indeed wonder if he had really existed and if any of this had happened. She would always have slight scars on her hands to look at, to remind her if she forgot to lock her door at night or close the window through which the wind came and stirred the curtains, but there was no longer a scar in her soul, just a numb sense of finality; and a sense of beginning. She was ready to start living a real life.

About Venti Editions

In early 2017, we introduced the Venti line of Clocktower Books. These are the new books, driven by digital technology, and no longer locked into the old technology-based definitions of short stories (print magazine) or novels (print book).

Venti means Twenty or Winds. Either way, a new wind is blowing (to quote Bob Dylan), and the middle length is open to anything longer than an old-fashioned short story and shorter than an old-fashioned print book (60,000 words on up).

Naturally, we'll pass along the great pricing you expect in a shorter, faster, better Venti Print edition. That term, by the way, we borrowed from a NASA concept—didn't work out so well for the space program, but works great for Venti publishing. To the stars, then!

About Clocktower Books

Our excellent authors include Renee Horowitz (*Pharmacy Sleuth Trilogy*); Robin Marchesi (*A Small Journal of Heroin Addiction*, a prose-poem autobiography in the finest post-Beat tradition); Deborah Cannon (*Raven Trilogy*); and others including our Teenage Novelist/Poet. To learn about our latest offerings, please visit:

www.clocktowerbooks.com

Clocktower Books, a pioneering Internet, e-book, and San Diego small press publisher, launched in April 1996 by publishing the world's first entire (not partial) proprietary (not public domain) novels (long works, industry standard) for reading online in HTML format (not for reading on portable media like CD-ROM, floppies, or other intermediary media). Some reviewers are confused and think Gutenberg did this first, but they specialize in public domain. We were the first (John Argo: Neon Blue, This Shoal of Space, Pioneers; John T. Cullen: The Generals of October) to publish proprietary novels as noted.

Clocktower Books Museum Site

You will find at the Museum Pages on our website a detailed history of our pioneering publishing house starting from 1996—including references and documentation (ever a work in progress).

museum.clocktowerbooks.com

From 1998 to 2007, Clocktower Books also published what was, during its decade-long run, the world's first professional Web-only (online) magazine of speculative and dark fiction (or SFFH). We published new authors as well as officers and top names of the Science Fiction Writers of America (SFWA); more on our pioneering work at the Science Fiction Encyclopedia online (look under Far Sector).

Our magazine's major names over the years included Deep Outside SFFH and Far Sector SFFH. We published many nominees or later awardees of the Hugo, Nebula, Sturgeon, and other global awards including British, Canadian, and Australian. The leading SF magazine historian Mike Ashley (Liverpool University Press) has stated he will recognize our pioneering magazine in the final volume of his authoritative SF magazine histories. We are mentioned in the SF Encyclopedia.

John Argo and Clocktower Books Present

Stunning and poetic far-future history by John Argo in the tradition of Cordwainer Smith's Classic Norstrilia and other tales of the Instrumentality.

A Science Fiction Novel in the Empire of Time Series

Star Clans of Corduwaine

Acclaimed Author whose works include the Empire of Time and DarkSF Series

Clocktower Books – San Diego

Jean-Thomas Cullen and Clocktower Books Present

Stop By: A sentimental, clean romantic story set in contemporary Connecticut. A young war widow has become a Sleeping Beauty, stung by the loss of her soldier husband, and works as a librarian in the tiny town of Emery. One hot summer day, just looking for a cool spot while his car is fixed, Prince Charming stops by in the form of a young millionaire who has suffered a painful divorce and isn't really looking for love. Neither is she. But old Cupid shoots them both with his arrows, and the ground moves beneath their feet...

Valley of Seven Castles: Progressive Thriller

Set in tomorrow's Europe, in a world gone global and run as one big feudal state by a thousand zillionaire families, here is the world's first progressive thriller. A U.S. Army deserter running from a crime he didn't commit, and a young California woman who sold herself into a modern form of five-year slavery to pay her mother's final hospital bills, are on the run. With them they carry the plans for a new warplane fuselage that must not fall into the wrong hands. Chasing them from Paris to Luxembourg is the Chinese billionaire who murdered a young Luxembourg engineer in London and wants his toy back. In the spirit of John Buchan's 1915 *The Thirty-Nine Steps* as well as Alfred Hitchcock's 1935 movie version *The 39 Steps*, plus a big surprise (see Thrillerology in the novel). Add to that the pace of the 2002 thriller movie The Bourne Identity starring Matt Damon and Franka Potente, based on a 1970 thriller novel by Robert Ludlum, and you have a first-class read.

Valley of Seven Castles
A Luxembourg Thriller by John T. Cullen

PROGRESSIVE THRILLERS SERIES

Also By John Argo: YANAPOP

Here's a thriller unlike anything you've ever read. Think of the dark comedy movie After Hours (Martin Scorsese, all-star cast) which is considered one of the funniest (and craziest) films ever made. We agree. Think of Linda Fiorentino in The Last Seduction, Jack Lemmon in The Out-of-Towners, and how about Thomas Pynchon's classic novel The Crying of Lot 49. YANAPOP (stands for Young Adult, New Adult, Participating Older Persons) is the name of a giant (fictional) entertainment corporation in Los Angeles. It's the love story of Martin Brown and Chloë Setreal, and how Martin became Odysseus in his insane and dangerous journey to reach his Penelope.

Nonfiction by John T. Cullen: Dead Move

John T. Cullen, a San Diego author and scholar (BA, BBA, MS) applies his journalistic and historical expertise to solve a long-standing true crime. During Thanksgiving Week 1892, a stylish young woman (about 24) officially called The Beautiful Stranger by the Hotel del Coronado near San Diego, checked in under a false name and died a violent, mysterious death a few days later. Her case became a national sensation full of notoriety overnight because of allegations of affairs with men in high places. It was a Victorian scandal of epic proportions, resulting in the famous ghost legend at the hotel. John T. Cullen, basing his research entirely on true history (no ghosts were harmed), provides the first ever plausible explanation of what really happened—including a coverup of global proportions. See also Lethal Journey, the noir gaslight mystery thriller he wrote to dramatize Dead Move, on which Lethal Journey is closely based.

Coronado Mystery

by
JOHN T. CULLEN
2 great books in 1

Dead Move &
Lethal Journey

1892 GASLIGHT MYSTERY
San Diego's notorious true crime
enigma solved - ghost legend
THE BEAUTIFUL STRANGER
* her violent mysterious death *

Thriller by John T. Cullen: Lethal Journey

Closely based on his nonfictional scholarly analysis of the 1892 true crime (*Dead Move*) here is a dramatization treated as a gaslight era noir suspense thriller.

Ray Bradbury Loved This One:

Ray Bradbury wrote a personal fan mail note to John T. Cullen in January 2008, praising this little gem, a novel that is a tribute both to Charles Dickens' classic A Christmas Carol, and to Ray Bradbury's dark but playful fantasies.

Lots More Where These Came From...

Please visit the website of Clocktower Books for a full listing of our exciting fiction and nonfiction books, articles, and short works by a variety of talented authors.

www.clocktowerbooks.com

Look for Upcoming Great Venti Editions

Venti means twenty. The intermediate length of Venti edition may run anywhere from about 20,000 to 30,000 words. Take our word for it!